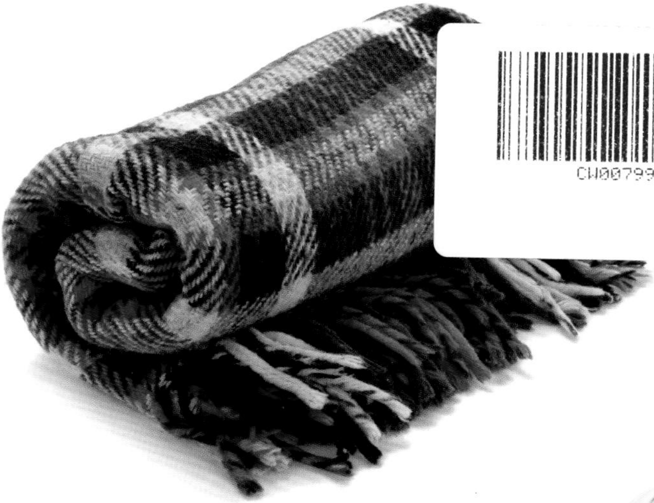

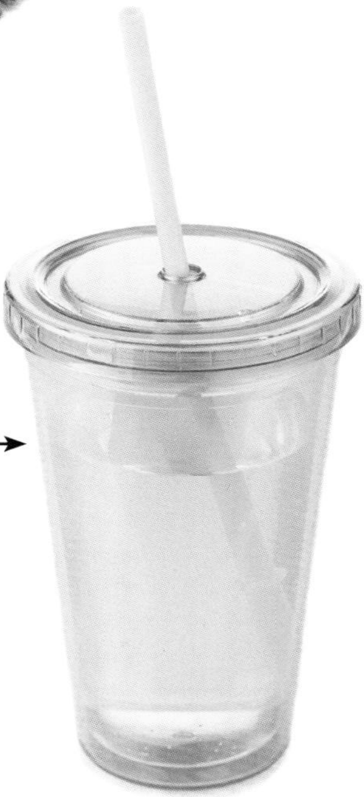

Pack a rug and a cup.

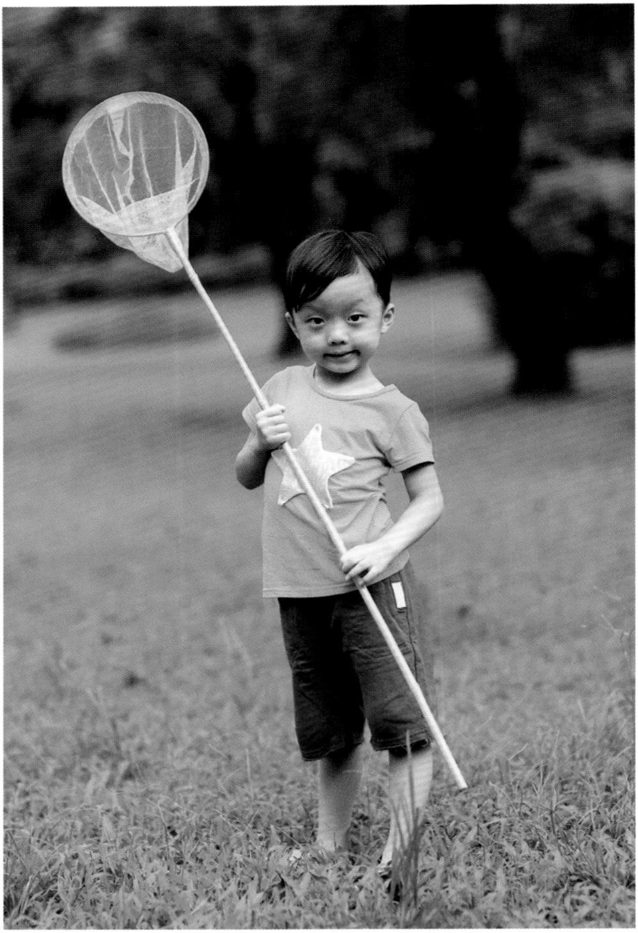

Get a net.

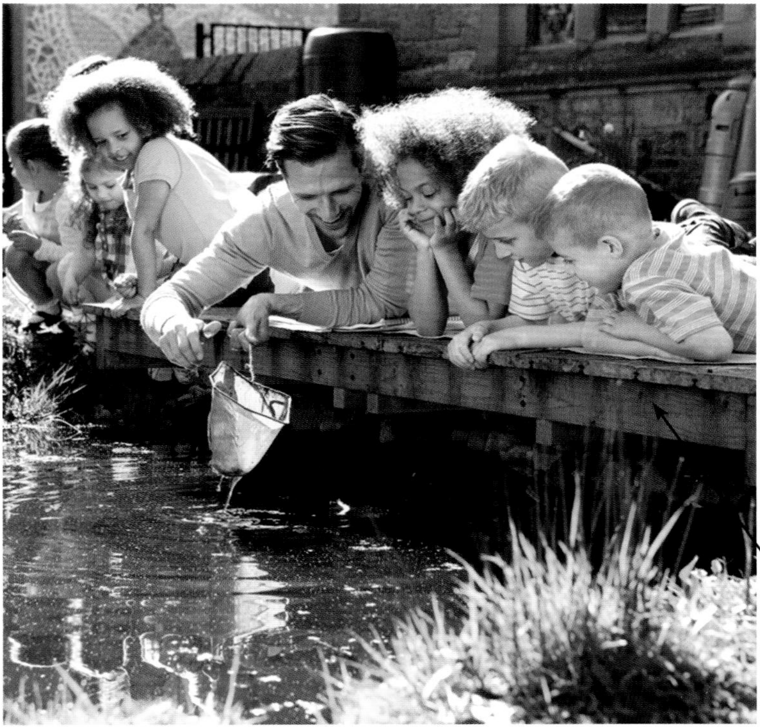

Dip a net in.

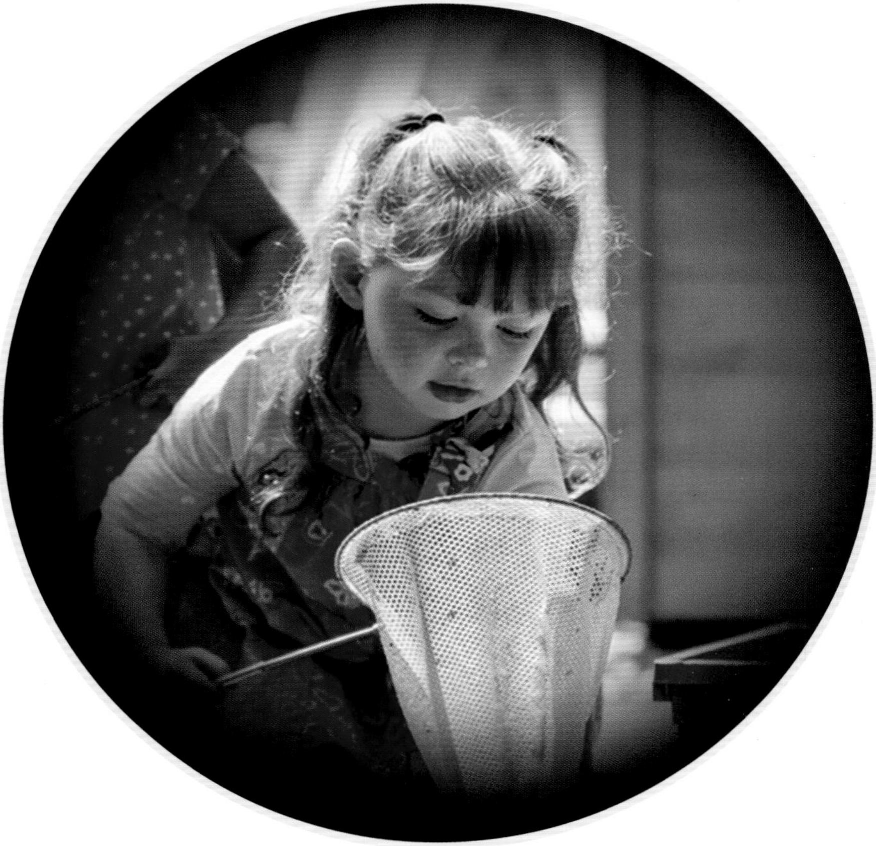

Pick it up.

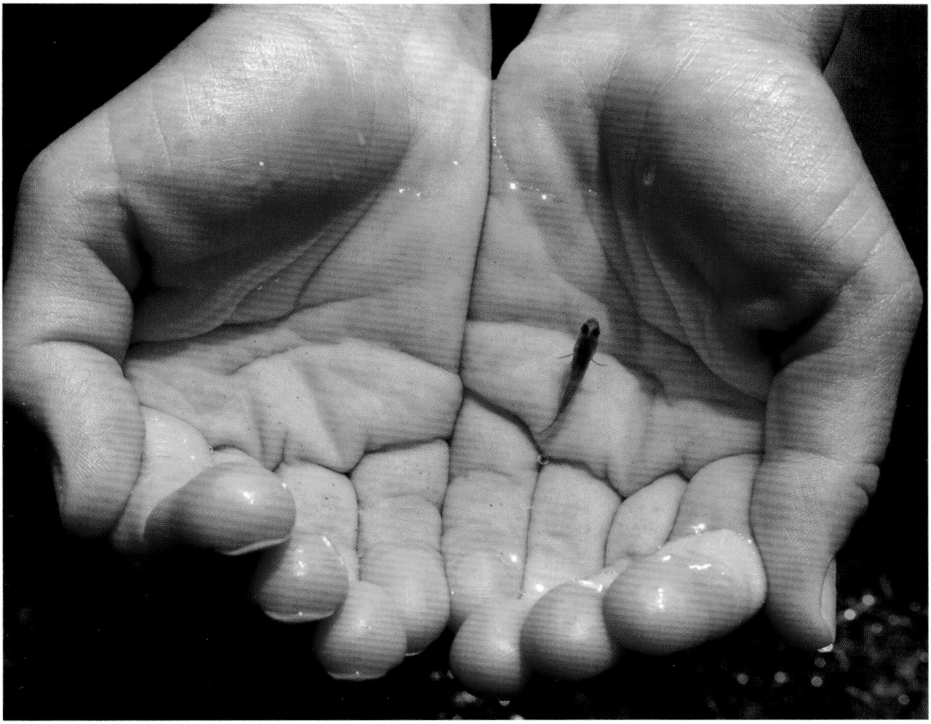

Pop it back.

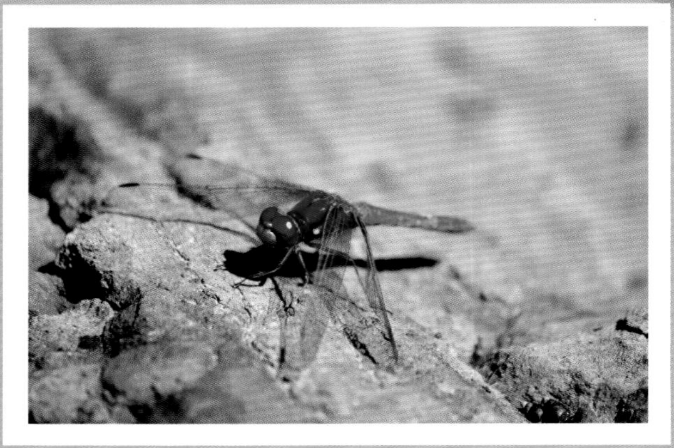

a red bug on mud

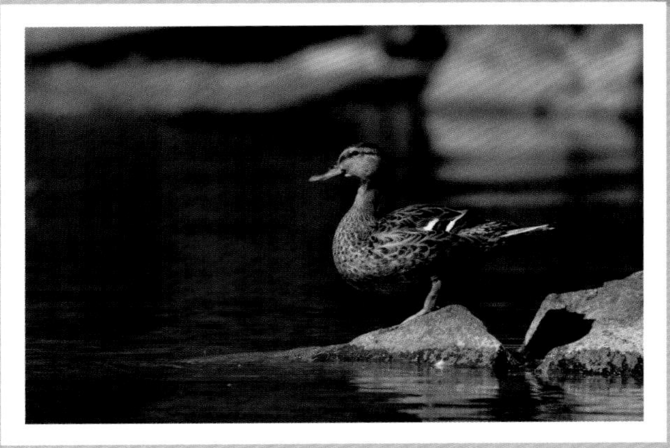

a duck on a rock

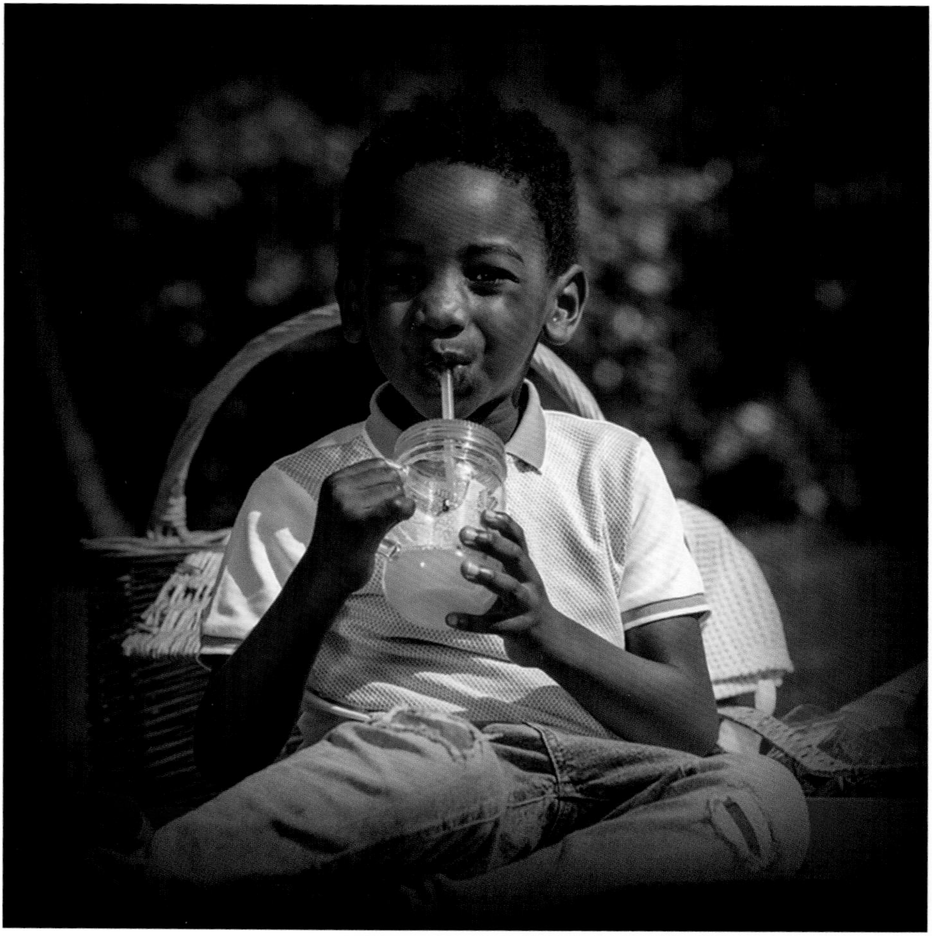

Sit and sip.